Bobby Ba

Little Joe Otter

"COME ON, CHILDREN!" CRIED MRS. JOE.
Frontispiece. See page 42.

BURGESS TRADE QUADDIES MARK

Smiling Pool Series

Little
Joe Otter

By

THORNTON W. BURGESS

With Illustrations by
HARRISON CADY

Grosset & Dunlap

PUBLISHERS   NEW YORK

PRINTED IN THE UNITED STATES OF AMERICA

BY ARRANGEMENT WITH LITTLE, BROWN AND COMPANY

CONTENTS

CONTENTS

ILLUSTRATIONS

CHAPTER I

LITTLE JOE OTTER SPRINGS A SURPRISE

Folks are n't so sure about you when
You spring surprises now and then.

Little Joe Otter.

OF all the little Quaddies who
live in the Green Meadows, the
Smiling Pool and the Green Forest,
none is more surprising than Little
Joe Otter. He is full of surprises, is Little Joe. He has a way
of suddenly bobbing up and just
as suddenly disappearing, which
makes him one of the hardest of all
the little people to get acquainted
with. Just when you think there

is no one around, up bobs Little
Joe and gives you a surprise.
Just when you are watching him,
down he goes and you never see
him again.

And when you are acquainted
with him, he is just as surprising.
He is full of pranks and dearly
loves to play. He is a wonderful swimmer, as no one knows better than those who live in the
Smiling Pool. At times he is a
great traveler in spite of his short
legs, and he knows more of the
Great World than most of his
neighbors. In winter he swims
under the ice and makes slippery
slides down the snowy banks. In
summer he makes slippery slides
on muddy banks.

It is his wonderful swimming power which enables him to do many things in secret. You see, when he disappears under the water, his neighbors on land have no way of knowing where he goes or what he does. Billy Mink and Jerry Muskrat are the only ones who know much about Little Joe Otter, and even they do not know as much as they might, or as they think they do.

Peter Rabbit had missed Little Joe Otter in the Smiling Pool this spring. He had asked Jerry Muskrat and Billy Mink where Little Joe was.

"Oh!" replied Jerry Muskrat. "Probably he is on one of his foolish long journeys. What any one wants to leave the Smiling Pool for is more than I can understand. Probably if you go down to the Big River, you will find him fishing there."

Just then there was a sudden splash right behind Jerry Musk-rat. It was so sudden that it startled Jerry, and the first thing that Jerry does when he is startled is to dive. He did this time. When he came up, Peter Rabbit was still sitting on the bank of the Smiling Pool.

"What was it that frightened me?" asked Jerry.

Peter grinned. "I'm sure I don't know. All I saw was a splash in the water."

"Chuga-rum!" cried Grandfather

Frog in his deepest, gruffest voice. "If I know anything about it, it was Little Joe Otter himself. I think, Jerry Muskrat, if you go far enough up the Laughing Brook, you will find that Little Joe is up there and not down at the Big River. I saw something that looked to me very much like a dark form swimming under water in that direction."

"I don't believe it," replied Jerry. "Little Joe hasn't been in the Smiling Pool in ever and ever so long. It would be a good thing if Little Joe would settle down. He ought to have a house the same as I have. I never did believe there was any good in this roaming around."

Just then there were two splashes right where the Laughing Brook comes into the Smiling Pool. Peter and Grandfather Frog and Jerry looked hastily in that direction. Then they stared at each other.

"Did I or did n't I see double?" Peter demanded. "It looked to me much like two Little Joe Otters!"

"It looked to me very much the same way," said Jerry.

Grandfather Frog looked thoughtful. "I have a suspicion," said he, "that little Joe Otter is springing a surprise on us. Have any of you heard of a Mrs. Joe?"

Peter looked at Jerry and Jerry looked at Peter. "Do you suppose it can be true?" they both exclaimed together.

CHAPTER II

PETER RABBIT GOES LOOKING

If there are things you would find out
Just use your eyes and look about.

Little Joe Otter.

No one had ever heard of a
Mrs. Joe Otter, yet if there was n't
a Mrs. Joe how was it that Grandfather Frog and Peter Rabbit
and Jerry Muskrat, all three, had
seemed to see two little brown
heads where the Laughing Brook
comes into the Smiling Pool. For
a while they talked it over between themselves. Each was sure
that he had seen two. It was

only for a moment and then there was nothing to be seen. It was all very mysterious.

"There must be something the matter with our eyes," declared Jerry. "Little Joe is such an uneasy fellow that he never would be content to settle down with a home of his own. Besides, wherever would he have found Mrs. Joe, if there is one?"

"I don't know, but I'm going to find out," said Peter, hopping up. "I'm going to go right straight up the Laughing Brook and look for his home. If he's got one, I don't believe he can hide it from me." With this off started Peter, lipperty-lipperty-lip.

"Good luck to you, Peter. If

you find anything come back and tell us," shouted Jerry Muskrat.

Up the Laughing Brook went Peter. Now he had no more idea than the man in the moon what kind of a home Little Joe Otter would be likely to have. He knew that Jerry Muskrat has two kinds of homes — one a hole in a bank, and the other a house in the Smiling Pool. He knew that Paddy the Beaver builds the same kinds of homes, only better. He knew that Billy Mink sometimes makes his home in a hollow log and sometimes under an old pile of brush and sometimes in a hole under a stump. Billy is not particular as to where his home is.

But Peter did n't know where to look for Little Joe's home.

" He lives in the water even more than Billy Mink does, almost as much as Jerry Muskrat does, so I guess he probably has a home right close to the water," said Peter. Then another thought struck him. He remembered that Jerry Muskrat makes his entrance to his home in the bank under water where it cannot be seen from the shore. If Little Joe were to do the same thing, he, Peter, might just as well look for a needle in a haystack. However, Peter is not easily discouraged. He hopped along, up one bank of the Laughing Brook, looking and looking for holes. Every hole he came to he

examined with the greatest care.
He sniffed and sniffed at each one,
hoping to get a whiff of Little
Joe Otter. When he had gone a
long way up the Laughing Brook
he crossed it on an old log and
went back down the other side,
looking and looking just the
same.

But with all Peter's looking, he
did n't find a thing. More than
this, he saw no signs that Little
Joe Otter had been up the Laughing Brook for a long time. He
was just about to give up, discouraged, when in a deep little
pool he heard a splash. He turned
quickly. He was just in time to
see Little Joe Otter swimming
away with a fish in his mouth.

"Hi, Little Joe!" he called. "Are you living up this way?"

Little Joe grinned in spite of the fish in his mouth. "Certainly I am," said Little Joe. "Come call on me and meet Mrs. Joe."

With that Little Joe suddenly disappeared under water, and though Peter sat for a long, long time watching, he saw nothing more of Little Joe.

"Now however am I going to make a call when I don't know where to call?" muttered Peter, as he started for the dear Old Briar-patch. "Anyway, I have found out that there is a Mrs. Joe!" he added triumphantly.

CHAPTER III

LITTLE JOE OTTER'S HOME

No matter how you love to roam
There comes a time you want a home.

Little Joe Otter.

Now though Peter Rabbit did n't know it, he had walked right straight over the home of Little Joe Otter. Many other little forest people had walked over that home without guessing it. You see, Little Joe is just as smart in making a home as he is in everything else. Little Joe believes that a home is just for those who live there, and therefore that it is a secret which no one else should know. He had found Mrs. Joe far away on the Big River and had brought her back with him up the Laughing Brook to the Smiling Pool and through the Smiling Pool farther up the Laughing Brook to the place he had picked out for a home. They had come right through the Smiling Pool while Grandfather Frog was sitting on his green lily pad and Jerry Muskrat was sitting on the Big Rock talking to Peter Rabbit, who was sitting on the bank. Only once had they shown their little brown heads above the water, and that was when Peter and Jerry and Grandfather Frog had thought they saw double. You see, Mrs. Joe was

very, very shy, and so Little Joe
wanted her to become acquainted
with the Laughing Brook and her
new home before he introduced her
to his friends and neighbors.

The place he had chosen for a
home was close beside one of the
deepest pools in the Laughing
Brook. Growing close to the
bank was a big tree with spreading roots. The bank was steep
and mossy. All about grew the
Green Forest. It was very lovely
there. Also it was very quiet,
and you probably would have
called it very lonely. But it was
just such a place as Otters love.

"Oh!" cried Mrs. Joe, when she
saw it. "Is this where our home
is to be?"

"Yes, my dear," replied Little Joe. "That is, it is if you like it. I thought we could make our house with a back door between two of the roots of that old tree, and with a front door deep down under water. By and by, if we want, we can have a slippery slide down the bank. There are plenty of fish in the Laughing Brook and we are far enough in the Green Forest not to have visitors very often."

Mrs. Joe dived into the little pool. She was gone a long time and Little Joe waited on the bank anxiously. When she came up she looked very happy. "It is perfectly lovely!" she cried. "It is the finest place for a home I ever have seen. Let's begin to make it right away, Little Joe!"

Little Joe didn't wait for her to change her mind. He remembered how many times Polly Chuck had changed her mind before Johnny Chuck succeeded in getting her to let him dig their home under the old apple tree in the far corner of the Old Orchard. "We'll begin right off," said he. And that is just what they did do.

Now you know Little Joe Otter can stay under water a long time. Mrs. Joe showed him just where she wanted the front door, deep down under water. Then they took turns making a long, nice hallway, slanting up from that under-water doorway. When it was high enough to be wholly above water they made the nicest little room, and then began a doorway which would lead out between two roots of the big tree. At first they did n't open this doorway, because you see they had no need of it. They just made the hall and left the door closed, so there was n't a thing to show where their home was. When they wanted to go out, they just slid down their front hallway into the little pool and then swam clear across it before they came up. This was so that if any sharp eyes happened to see them, they never would guess where they had come from. When it was all done, they had just the best time ever.

CHAPTER IV

PETER RABBIT LEARNS BY SITTING STILL

By sitting still may much be learned
And thus be useful knowledge earned.

Little Joe Otter.

Do you know that you can learn things by sitting perfectly still? You can. That is, you can if you use your eyes and use your ears and all the other senses that Old Mother Nature has given you. Peter Rabbit discovered it quite by accident. You know how curious he is. It seems as if his curiosity never can be satisfied.

On the day that Little Joe Otter invited him to call at his home and then promptly disappeared, Peter could think of nothing but that home, and wonder where it was. Whenever he got the chance he went over to the Green Forest to look for Little Joe and his home. He had hopped up and down the banks of the Laughing Brook until his feet ached, and he was just as wise as before.

At last one day, he sat down just a little way from a great big tree with spreading roots near the bank of a little pool in the Laughing Brook. He was tired. Also he was discouraged. "I don't believe Little Joe has a home at all," he muttered. Then, because he was tired, he squatted down in a little brown heap and closed his eyes. How long he slept Peter never knew. When he awoke it was very, very still there in the Green Forest. He felt rested and therefore in a better frame of mind. He decided he would sit there a little longer and enjoy his beautiful surroundings before going back to the dear Old Briar-patch.

Now when Peter sits perfectly still, he is very hard to see. He looks like nothing so much as a little brown heap of dead leaves, and that was the way he was looking then. But all the time he was watching this way and that way to see what he could discover.

Quite without any warning at all there was a rustling of leaves between two of the roots of the old tree a little way off. Peter didn't have to turn his head to look. You see, his eyes are set so far back that he can see without turning his head. What he saw made him catch his breath and open his eyes wider than ever. What do you think it was? Why it was a little brown baby rolling and tumbling in the leaves!

Peter had never seen a baby like it before. While he was watching and wondering whose baby it could be, another joined it. They tumbled and rolled over each other. They played tug-of-war with a little stick, each holding one end. They made believe bite each other. It was very rough play, but the rougher it was the better they seemed to like it. Peter watched them for a long time. Then, because he had a cramp in one of his feet, he moved ever so little, and in doing so he rustled the leaves. Instantly the two brown babies disappeared as if the earth had swallowed them up. Peter waited, but they did n't appear again.

At last his curiosity proved too much for him. He hopped over to the spreading roots of the old tree and there was the nicest little doorway he had ever seen. He knew then where the two brown babies had disappeared.

"I wonder," muttered Peter, "whose babies those were. I wonder —" A sudden thought popped into his head. It made him jump right up in the air. "Do you suppose that those could have been Little Joe Otter's babies?" he exclaimed right out loud to nobody in particular. Then, because he was so full of his discovery, he scampered away to the dear Old Briar-patch to tell Mrs. Peter all about it.

One morning he saw Mrs. Joe out with the two
babies. *Page* 28.

CHAPTER V

A SCHOOL IN THE GREEN FOREST

It is Old Mother Nature's rule
For every one to go to school.
Little Joe Otter.

PETER RABBIT could not keep
away from the Green Forest. No,
Sir, he could n't. He just could n't
do it. You see, having discovered
those two queer, brown babies
under a big tree on the bank of
the Laughing Brook, he just had
to go back there every chance he
could get to watch them. So,
whenever he could, he slipped over
there to watch. He kept as still

as still could be, and not once did those little brown babies suspect that he was near. Every day they came out to play, but at the least sound they would disappear in that snug home, the doorway of which was between the roots of the big tree.

After a little Peter discovered that there was a school in the Green Forest, just as there was a school at Johnny Chuck's home in the Old Orchard, and another where Danny Meadow Mouse had his home on the Green Meadows. You see, wherever there are babies there has to be a school. This is one of the laws of Old Mother Nature. Peter had been quite right when he had guessed that

these babies were the children of
Little Joe Otter. At first they
seemed to do nothing but tumble
over each other and play; it was
very rough play, the roughest play,
that Peter ever had seen. He
did n't guess that in that play
those two brown babies were
learning something, but they
were. They were learning how
to use their legs and teeth and
bodies.

At first Peter had seen nothing
of Little Joe Otter or Mrs. Joe,
but he noticed that at the least
rustle of a leaf the two brown
babies disappeared in their home,
and by this he knew that they had
been taught that great law of all
the little wild people, which is that

safety is the first and most important lesson to be learned.

Then one morning he saw Mrs. Joe out with the two babies, and they were having a grand frolic. Mrs. Joe would get hold of one end of a stick and the two little Otters would get hold of the other end of the stick and try to pull it away from her. In this way they were learning how to grow strong and to take care of themselves.

Then Mrs. Joe took them a little way into the woods. It just happened that Reddy Fox had been along that way the night before. She showed them his tracks and made them smell of them, and when she did this she growled, and thus they knew that Reddy was an enemy to be watched out for.

Later, right in the midst of one of their grand frolics, Sammy Jay suddenly began to scream. Peter knew perfectly well what that scream meant. He knew by the noise that Sammy had discovered somebody in the Green Forest. Of course Mrs. Otter knew, and right away she chased her two brown babies into their home and followed them. Thus they learned that a screaming Jay is a warning to watch out for danger.

One thing puzzled Peter very much. He knew that Little Joe Otter lives in the water most of the time, and that of course Mrs. Joe does the same thing. "I wonder why those youngsters are not taught to swim," thought Peter. "I should suppose that a swimming lesson would be one of the very first things they would get."

Peter puzzled over this a great deal as one day followed another and still the Otter babies never once went near the water. They grew fast, and had the very best times ever were, but always on the land. In fact, Peter suspected by the way they acted that they did n't like the water any better than he did, and you know he does n't like it at all. Mrs. Otter, and sometimes Little Joe, brought them fish to eat, and sometimes their mother took them on little short hunting trips, but always on the land. It was too much for Peter; it seemed to him that those Otter children were being brought up altogether wrong.

CHAPTER VI

THE FIRST SWIMMING LESSON

You 'll never learn to float on sand,
Nor swim by staying on the land.

Little Joe Otter.

ONE morning Peter Rabbit was a little late in getting over to the home of Little Joe Otter. When he got there, there was not a sign of the two brown Otter children at the doorway of their home between the roots of the big tree. " It must be," thought Peter, " that they have gone off hunting. I wonder if I can find them if I look for them."

Just then his ears caught the sound of splashing in the Laughing Brook. Very, very carefully Peter crept over where he could see what was going on. Such a funny sight as it was! There in the water were Little Joe and Mrs. Joe, diving and swimming and splashing as only they can. On the bank were the two Otter children, watching with their eyes round with wonder, and a great longing. At the same time it was very clear to Peter that those two youngsters were afraid of the water. Little Joe and Mrs. Joe kept calling to them to come in, but they would n't.

No, Sir, those little Otters would n't more than wet their feet.

Mrs. Joe swam over to where they were and coaxed them, as only a mother can. It was of no use. All the coaxing in the world could n't overcome their fear of the water. Then she pretended to be very angry, and she ordered them to follow her. They whimpered and cried, but not one step into the water would they go. Then she tried making fun of them, but she was no more successful than before.

They were afraid. Yes, Sir, they were afraid. There was no doubt about it. Peter does n't like the water himself, but when he has to he can swim. He could n't remember ever having been as much afraid of the water

as those two Otter children, not
even when he was a very little
fellow. And that seemed funny,
too. In fact, Peter could n't
understand it at all. Here were
two babies whose father and
mother were among the best
swimmers in the world, and yet
they could n't get their two youngsters into the water.

Finally, with a great deal of
coaxing, Mrs. Otter got one of them
to take a ride on her back.
Then she gave the other a ride.
For a long time they swam around
and around, and had a beautiful
time. The babies liked this. You
see, they felt perfectly safe, and
it was great fun to be carried
about, here and there and every-

where. Then, without the least bit of warning, while both babies were on her back Mrs. Joe dived. Now of course when she did this, it carried the two babies right under water, and the minute they went under water they let go and came to the top.

My, my, my, what a frightened pair they were! They blew the water out of their noses, and both began to whimper and cry. But at the same time both began to paddle as fast as ever they could.

Little Joe and Mrs. Joe popped their round brown heads out of water and swam just ahead of the two babies. The two babies did their very best to get on the backs of Little Joe and Mrs. Joe. But

the latter kept just out of their
reach. Then one of the babies
stopped crying. He had discovered something; he had discovered
that he was swimming, and that
swimming was really great fun.
Somehow that water did n't seem
so dreadful any more. Then the
other discovered the same thing.
They had had their first swimming
lesson and had found that mother
and father were right after all ; the
water would n't hurt them. When
at last they scrambled up on the
shore and shook the water from
their little brown coats, their eyes
were shining with pride and excitement.

CHAPTER VII

GREAT FUN ON A SLIPPERY SLIDE

Many lessons learned in play
You'll find a use for every day.
Little Joe Otter.

OF course Peter Rabbit hadn't
been able to keep to himself the
fact that Little Joe Otter had a
home and wife and two lively
babies. He just *had* to tell the
other Quaddies. Those who dared,
and could go so far into the Green
Forest, visited the little pool in
the Laughing Brook. But they
were very quiet about it. You
see, though they were not exactly

bashful, they had a feeling that Little Joe might not like visitors, and most of them had a great deal of respect for Little Joe's sharp, strong teeth. No one willingly quarrels with Little Joe Otter. Sammy Jay, of course, had nothing to fear in the tree tops, but soon discovered that as soon as it was known that he was about, there was nothing to see. So after that Sammy came silently and took the greatest care to keep hidden in the thickest part of a hemlock tree, but one from which he could peep forth and see all that was going on below. And so Sammy watched the merriest sliding party he ever had seen.

Sammy had flown over there very

early that morning. So far, he had had no more than a glimpse of the Otter children. He knew all about the children of Peter Rabbit and Johnny Chuck and Danny Meadow Mouse. He had watched them learn the lessons which it was most important for them to learn if they would live to grow up. He had watched them at play as well as at school. But of the ways of Little Otters he knew nothing at all.

As he sat in the tall hemlock tree and looked down he felt quite excited. Somehow he had a feeling — he didn't know why — that he was going to see something worth seeing. So he waited patiently. It was very beautiful

there in the Green Forest. The
Laughing Brook was dimpling and
smiling where the sunbeams crept
through the tree tops to kiss it,
and it sang merrily as it hurried
on to the Smiling Pool. Some-
where deeper in the Green Forest
was Melody the Wood Thrush
pouring out his joy in silver notes
that made glad the hearts of
all who heard. Listening, Sammy
was almost jealous. "If I had
as beautiful a voice as that to
go with my beautiful coat there
would be no one in the world to
compare with me," he thought,
quite forgetting that a beautiful
character is far more to be desired
than a beautiful voice or a beautiful coat. A splash in the still

little pool below him reminded him what he was waiting for. Eagerly he peered down. Little Joe Otter was just swimming towards the shore, and at the top of the bank where it was steepest and smoothest were Mrs. Joe and the two Otter children.

Mrs. Joe stretched herself flat, gave a kick with her feet, and away she slid, headfirst down the bank and splash into the water. The two children poked their heads over the edge of the bank and it was very plain that they wanted to follow but did n't quite dare.

"Come on, children!" cried Mrs. Joe, splashing and diving and swimming round and round.

But still the youngsters were

afraid. By this time Little Joe had climbed back up the bank. "This is the way to do it," said he, and down the bank he went, splash into the pool.

One of the youngsters stretched himself out at the top of the slide as he had seen Little Joe and Mrs. Joe do, but he could n't quite make up his mind to kick off. Right then something so funny happened that Sammy Jay nearly gave himself away by laughing right out. The other little Otter just gave the first one a push and down he went. You see, when he once started he could n't stop. He clawed and tried frantically to stop, but down he went, splash into the water. It was very, very funny. It was still more funny to see his face when he came up and shook the water from his eyes. He was proud and excited and he had lost all fear. In another minute he was scrambling up the bank to try it again.

He had gone down the slippery slide five times before the other had found courage enough to try it. And then such fun! First Little Joe Otter, then Mrs. Joe, and after her the two youngsters, one right at the heels of another, slid down and splashed into the little pool until they were so tired that they just had to lie down to rest. Never was there such fun. Sammy Jay was almost envious again.

CHAPTER VIII

FARMER BROWN'S BOY HAS NO LUCK

Oh, who would not a-fishing go — a-fishing
    go — a-fishing go?
  Oh, who would not a-fishing go all on a
    summer's day?
Oh, who would not a-fishing go — a-fishing
    go — a-fishing go?
  Oh, who would not a-fishing go where
    fishes sport and play?

Little Joe Otter.

FARMER BROWN'S boy with his
rod and a can of worms was making his way to the Laughing Brook.
He felt good all over, did Farmer
Brown's boy. He felt good because it was the kind of a day to
make any one feel good. And he
felt good because it was a holiday

for him and he knew that he had earned it. He had worked hard in the hayfield for days and days, and in the cornfield and in the garden, and never once had he complained. You see, he knew that the work just had to be done. That morning at breakfast Farmer Brown had given him a surprise. It was such a splendid surprise! He had told him that that day was to be his very own in which to do just what he wanted to do. Do you wonder that he felt good all over?

The very first thing he thought of was fishing. He just *knew* that the speckled trout were waiting for him to catch them. And now he was on his way with a lunch in his pocket and joy in his heart, so much joy that it was bubbling out in the merriest of whistles. As he made his way through the Green Forest to the Laughing Brook, it seemed to him that all the little people he saw by the way were glad because he was glad.

Now there was a certain quiet pool deep in the Green Forest where Farmer Brown's boy was certain he would find hungry trout. He had n't the smallest doubt of it. More than once he had looked down in that clear pool and seen big trout there, and he was sure he would find them there now. So he headed straight for this particular pool. When he was near enough he put a fat worm on his hook and dropped it in the water.

He didn't doubt that it would be taken at once by a fat, hungry, speckled trout.

"I ought to catch at least three in this pool," said he to himself, and waited, keeping perfectly still. Nothing happened. Farmer Brown's boy moved the bait about in the most enticing way he knew how, and still nothing happened. He didn't get so much as a nibble.

"This is queer," muttered Farmer Brown's boy. "I never have had to wait so long for a bite in this pool before." He continued to keep perfectly still, as a good fisherman should, and waited patiently. Still there wasn't a nibble. Presently, having nothing else to do, he began to take note of things, the

trees, the flowers, the humming in-
sects and at last the opposite bank,
which was steep and smooth.

"Looks as if something had
been sliding down there," he muttered. "Wonder what it could
have been. Funny the trout don't
bite. I hate to give up, but guess
I'll have to. I'll go down to the
next pool and try my luck there."

So he trudged down to the next
pool and a pair of sharp eyes
watched him go. They were the
eyes of Sammy Jay, and Sammy
was chuckling under his breath.
You see, he knew why Farmer
Brown's boy had caught no fish.
The pool which he had just left
was the very pool in the bank of
which Little Joe Otter and Mrs.

Otter had their home, and now there were no fat trout there. Little Joe and Mrs. Joe had caught all of them. They are especially fond of trout.

But Farmer Brown's boy knew nothing of this. In fact, he knew very little about Little Joe Otter anyway. So he trudged on, sure that he would have better luck in the next pool. Sammy Jay followed, still chuckling. He seemed to find something a great joke.

"There are smarter fishermen in this brook than you, and I would n't give much for all the fish you will catch," he remarked to no one in particular. But he was looking at Farmer Brown's boy, who still had no luck.

CHAPTER IX

A FAMILY FISHING PARTY

'Tis vain to sit and wish and wish
When fishing where there are no fish.

Little Joe Otter.

FARMER BROWN'S boy had n't had one bite, not one teeny, weeny nibble, and he really did n't know what to make of it. Many times had he fished in the Laughing Brook but never before with quite such bad luck as this.

"Fishy, fishy, here's a worm!
Watch how he will twist and squirm!
Bite him first before you look
To see if he is on a hook."

Farmer Brown's boy said this over twice as he tossed his bait

into the second little pool. Then
he waited. He waited and waited
and waited! All good fishermen
wait and wait and wait. To catch
fish patience is as necessary as bait.
So Farmer Brown's boy waited.
Nothing happened; nothing at all.

"I wonder if some one has been
here before me and caught all the
trout," thought he. "I did n't get
a nibble at the first pool and I
have n't had a nibble at this pool.
Guess I 'll have to move on."

So he moved on towards the
third pool a little farther down the
Laughing Brook. He had almost
reached it when he heard a splash
and then another splash. He put
down his rod and crept forward
very, very carefully, so as to make

no sound. When he could see the little pool clearly he caught his breath. Other fishermen *were* ahead of him. In fact, a family fishing party was right in that very pool and having better luck, much better luck, than he had had. The members of that party were catching fish, the very trout he had been so sure of catching when he started out. These were the ones who had spoiled his fishing. Have you guessed who they were? They were Little Joe Otter, Mrs. Joe and the little Otters.

Farmer Brown's boy kept perfectly still and held his breath. He forgot all about his own fishing. He had seen Little Joe only once or twice before, and then had caught only a glimpse of his brown head in the Smiling Pool. Of course he had never seen Mrs. Joe or the two children.

Little Joe dived. He was gone so long that Farmer Brown's boy began to wonder what had become of him. Suddenly his brown head popped up and in his mouth was a beautiful, speckled trout, a trout that Farmer Brown's boy would have been delighted to have caught.

"Gee!" exclaimed Farmer Brown's boy under his breath.

Little Joe swam with the trout straight over to where the two little Otters were waiting on a big flat stone at the edge of the water, fairly dancing with excitement.

Just before he reached them, Little Joe dropped that fish. It could still swim, though not very fast.

Splash! The two young Otters were in the water after it, each eager to be the one to catch it. They were clumsy and overeager, and you know overeagerness often is quite as bad as being too slow. Each got in the way of the other. The fish twisted and turned and they tried to follow. At last, one of them made a lucky dash and proudly turned towards the bank with the fish in his mouth. Very proud he looked. The other swam after and tried to take the fish away from him. It looked very much as if there might be a fight right there in that little pool in the Laughing Brook. But just then Mrs. Joe interfered. She swam in between the two and pushed the unsuccessful one away. He went off by himself and sulked while the other dragged his prize out on a rock and began to eat.

A few minutes later Mrs. Joe caught another trout and this she carried to the little Otter who had none. When she let the fish go, it could swim only a little and so the young Otter had no trouble in catching it. Farmer Brown's boy wondered if it was just chance that those fish were alive, or if they had been kept so purposely to give the young Otters a lesson in fishing. I wonder too. Don't you?

CHAPTER X

A YOUNG FISHERMAN IS CAUGHT

The heedless young who disobey
Will for their folly have to pay.
                    Little Joe Otter.

FARMER BROWN'S boy watched the family fishing party until it moved on to the next pool. Then he remembered his own fishing and the fat trout he had promised to bring back for supper that night.

"Now I understand why I haven't had a bite," he chuckled. "Little Joe Otter and his family got started earlier than I did. They are welcome to all they have caught, for the fun of seeing those young Otters get their first fishing lesson is worth more to me than any fish could be. But I can't allow them to get *all* the fish. I could frighten them away, but I don't want to do that. No, Sir, I don't want to make them afraid of me. I know what I'll do; I'll circle around through the woods and get ahead of them."

So Farmer Brown's boy tramped around through the Green Forest until he reached the Laughing Brook again at a point where he felt sure of being ahead of the Otter fishing party. In a minute there was a sharp tug at his line and presently he pulled out a silvery, speckled trout. Then

Farmer Brown's boy forgot all about everything but fishing.

Now it just happened that that very morning Old Man Coyote had taken it into his head to visit the Laughing Brook and see what was going on there. It may be that in the back of that shrewd head of his was an idea there might be some helpless young babies or headstrong and careless young children of one kind or another who would furnish him with a tender and easily gotten breakfast. Anyway, he was going up the Laughing Brook and Farmer Brown's Boy was going down the Laughing Brook. Of course they met. However, Farmer Brown's boy didn't know it. He didn't know a thing about it. You see, he was so intent on fishing that he had no eyes for anything but the water and his fishing line. So he didn't see Old Man Coyote. But Old Man Coyote saw him and lifted his lips from his long, strong teeth in a most unpleasant manner as he sneaked past through the brush.

"Probably he has frightened everybody along the Laughing Brook," grumbled Old Man Coyote bitterly, as he went on his way.

But he had gone only a short distance after passing Farmer Brown's boy when his sharp ears heard a faint splash in a little pool just ahead. Instantly he dropped flat on his stomach and began to crawl forward an inch at a time, his eyes blazing with eagerness and his pointed ears cocked forward. Presently he saw Little Joe Otter and Mrs. Joe swimming, and a great disappointment swept over him. He knew that they were far too smart to be caught by him.

A moment later he saw the two young Otters. All his disappointment was forgotten and the eager look returned to his eyes. He couldn't imagine anything more to his liking than young Otter. His mouth watered. He licked his lips hungrily. Inch by inch he crept nearer. One of the young Otters climbed up the bank almost in front of him. Old Man Coyote wriggled nearer. He brought his hind feet under him, ready for a quick spring. Then he waited. He wanted that young Otter, but he was too crafty to risk a fight with Little Joe Otter and Mrs. Joe unless he had to. So he waited.

Presently Little Joe and Mrs. Joe called the two children and started down the Laughing Brook. The young Otter in the water obeyed instantly, but the one on the bank did n't. He was tired and he wanted to rest. The others could go if they wanted to, for they would n't go far and he could soon catch up with them. He rather liked the idea of being left alone. It made him feel more independent. There was nothing to fear. So he sat still and watched the others disappear around a turn in the Laughing Brook. When they were out of sight he chuckled. He thought himself very smart.

A very tiny noise behind him, the rustle of a leaf, caused him to turn his head. He had just time to get a glimpse of fierce, yellow eyes and gleaming teeth. Then the paws of Old Man Coyote landed on him. He was caught!

CHAPTER XI

SAMMY JAY CALLS FARMER BROWN'S BOY

In danger there is good excuse
For putting any tongue to use.

Little Joe Otter.

THE foolish little Otter, who had n't minded his father and mother but had remained behind on the bank of the little pool in the Laughing Brook, did n't have time to even squeal before Old Man Coyote had him. Old Man Coyote did n't kill him at once, as he might have done with one crunch of his great jaws. He wanted to play with him a little first.

Now, though Old Man Coyote thought that no one saw him, some one did. It was Sammy Jay. Sammy had been following the Otter family, keeping very still and taking the greatest pains to keep out of sight himself. You see, he was very much interested in those Otter children and he thought it great fun to watch them having their first lessons in fishing. So he was right where he could see perfectly what happened. The instant Old Man Coyote sprang from his hiding-place Sammy knew that the little Otter had n't a chance in the world unless he could do something. Right away he remembered Farmer Brown's boy fishing just a little farther down the Laughing Brook. "Perhaps," thought Sammy, "if I scream loud enough and long enough, he will come to see what all the fuss is about."

So Sammy opened his mouth and began to scream at the top of his lungs. "Thief! Thief! Thief!" he screamed, flying down just over Old Man Coyote's head.

Old Man Coyote looked up and snarled angrily. "Stop your noise!" he snapped. "This is none of your business."

"Thief! Thief! Thief!" screamed Sammy louder than ever.

Now the very instant that Sammy began to scream Little Joe Otter and Mrs. Joe, who were just around a turn in the Laughing Brook, knew that an enemy was near. For the first time they missed the little Otter who had remained behind. Little Joe did n't wait a second. He started back as fast as he could swim, which is very fast indeed. Mrs. Joe followed as soon as she had seen that the other little Otter was in a safe hiding-place.

Old Man Coyote was still snarling at Sammy Jay when he saw Little Joe coming, and behind him Mrs. Joe. He knew then that he was to have a fight, but he had no intention of giving up that little Otter. He backed away, dragging the little Otter with him and showing all his great teeth in ugly snarls. Meanwhile Sam-

my Jay kept up his screaming.
Of course Farmer Brown's boy
heard it. He stopped fishing to
listen. He knows the ways of
Sammy Jay, does Farmer Brown's
boy.

"Something going on back there,"
he muttered. "Wonder what it is.
Sammy does n't scream like that
unless he is terribly excited. Guess
I 'll have to see what it all
means."

He laid his rod down, leaving
the bait in the water. Very care-
fully he tiptoed back to where
Sammy was making such a racket.
He was just in time to see Little
Joe and Mrs. Joe rushing at Old
Man Coyote, who was growling
and snarling, while with his two

fore feet he held down the whimper-
ing little Otter. Farmer Brown's
boy did n't stop to think. He
just opened his mouth and yelled.
Then picking up a stick he rushed
forward.

Old Man Coyote did n't wait
for him to get there. At the
sound of that yell he jumped as
if he had been shot. Then he
turned and vanished like a shadow
in the brush. Little Joe Otter
and Mrs. Joe had been almost as
much frightened as Old Man Coyote, and they ran too. But they
did n't run far. Oh, my, no!
Their love was too strong for that.
They dived into the little pool,
but almost at once their brown
heads appeared again, as they

turned to see what new danger threatened their darling.

As for the latter, he was too badly frightened to move. He growled feebly in a very frightened way as Farmer Brown's boy picked him up.

" You poor little thing," said Farmer Brown's boy gently. " I would n't hurt you for the world."

But the little Otter could n't understand a word and just shivered with fear. At first Farmer Brown's boy thought that he would take the little fellow home for a pet. Then he looked down into the little pool straight into the eyes of Mrs. Joe, and he saw there such a look of anxious love and longing that he marched straight down to the edge of the water and gently put his little captive in it. Then he laughed and the laugh was good to hear as the little fellow dived and swam out to join his parents as fast as ever he could, and all three promptly disappeared. When he got back to where he had left his rod something was tugging at the line. It was the biggest trout he ever had caught.

CHAPTER XII

PETER RABBIT FINDS A QUEER TRAIL

Who seeks shall learn
And knowledge earn.

Little Joe Otter.

SUMMER had passed and winter had brought the first snow. Peter Rabbit likes snow. That is, he likes it if there is n't too much of it. Sometimes, when it is very deep, Peter has a hard time getting enough to eat. But when it is n't too deep he likes it. You see, Peter is full of curiosity, and when there is snow on the ground and it is n't crusted over, he is able to

learn many things about his neighbors. All he has to do is to follow their tracks to find out where
they have been and what they
have been doing.

So with the coming of the first
snow Peter hurried over to the
Green Forest, and as soon as he
got there he began to look for
tracks. The first he found were
the dainty little footprints of
Whitefoot the Wood Mouse.
They were almost as dainty as the
tracks of birds. He followed them
until they were joined by bigger
tracks. Then Peter stopped. He
suddenly lost interest. You see,
those bigger tracks he recognized
right away. They were the footprints of Reddy Fox. Peter

decided that this was no place for him, for he knew that those footprints were made only a very short time before.

So away went Peter in quite another direction. Presently he found footprints very like his own, only very much bigger. They were the footprints of his cousin, Jumper the Hare. "I haven't seen Cousin Jumper for a long time, so I guess I'll see if I can catch up with him," thought Peter.

He hurried, lipperty-lipperty-lip, following the trail of Jumper. It wound this way and that between the trees, and crossed and recrossed. Gradually it led towards the Laughing Brook. Suddenly

Peter sat up and stared round-eyed at another trail that crossed the trail of Jumper. It was a queer trail. It was the queerest trail Peter ever had seen. There were footprints, but they were queer footprints. They were quite round, and following straight along with them was a little furrow in the snow. Peter guessed right away that this was made by a tail. That would mean that the maker of the tracks had short legs.

Right away Peter forgot all about his cousin, Jumper the Hare. He was all curiosity to find out who had made this queer trail. He turned and followed it. Presently he came to where there was a gentle slope. There the footprints ended, but there was a long furrow clear down to the bottom of the slope. It was as if something had been pushed or dragged down the slope through the snow.

Peter hurried on. At the bottom of the slope he found the footprints again. He noticed that this trail always followed the easiest way. It never led over logs or stumps, but always around them. By and by he came to another of those long furrows in the snow. He stopped to study it. He scratched a long ear with a long hind foot. He scratched the other long ear with the other long hind foot. He was puzzled. He was very much puzzled. He didn't

know what to make of this long
furrow without any footprints.

"The only way to find out," he
decided, "is to catch up with the
one who has made this trail." So
he hurried on, lipperty-lipperty-lip.
And so at last he came to the top
of a steep bank at the bottom of
which ran the Laughing Brook.
Beginning at the top of this bank
was another one of those queer
furrows. It ended down below at
the edge of the water. Peter
looked across the Laughing Brook.
He could see no trail on the other
side. He looked everywhere, but
could see no signs of that trail. It
simply ended right there at the
Laughing Brook.

CHAPTER XIII

CURIOSITY IS SATISFIED

The curious to gratify,
You first will have to satisfy.

Little Joe Otter.

PETER RABBIT sat at the top of
the steep bank of the Laughing
Brook in the Green Forest, as puzzled a Rabbit as ever lived. The
queer trail he had followed ended
in this long furrow straight down
the steep bank to the water.
Peter had n't the least idea who
had made that queer trail. So he
sat there, staring all about rather
foolishly, and now and then

scratching a long ear with a long hind foot.

"Hello, Peter Rabbit! Isn't this great weather? Don't you just love it? I do," said a voice.

Peter stared all around, everywhere but in the right direction. Finally he just happened to look down in the black, cold water of the Laughing Brook. There in the very middle of it he saw a brown head with a pair of bright eyes full of mischief looking up at him.

"Little Joe Otter!" cried Peter. "Goodness, how you startled me! I couldn't tell where that voice came from. Yes, this is fine weather. I like it too. But I hope it won't get any colder."

"I don't care how cold it gets," declared Little Joe Otter. "By the way, what brings you over here to the Laughing Brook?"

That reminded Peter of the queer trail that had so puzzled him. "Some one, I haven't the least idea who, has been traveling about in the Green Forest, and has left the queerest trail I've ever seen," said he. "In parts of it there are no footprints at all; there is just a long furrow in the snow. Here is one of those furrows right down this bank."

Little Joe Otter's bright eyes twinkled. "That is queer," said he. "Now who under the sun do you suppose could have made it?"

"That's what I want to know,"

declared Peter. "But I guess I'll have to keep on wanting, for I don't see that trail coming out of the water anywhere."

"I'll have to have a little closer look at that. I'll join you in a minute," said Little Joe Otter.

He swam swiftly up the Laughing Brook and came out of the water where the bank was low. Then he made his way around up to where Peter was sitting. "That is a queer trail," said he, trying to keep his eyes from twinkling. "It looks to me as if some one had slid down there. I tell you what, Peter, let's slide down, too, and see how it seems."

"No, thank you," replied Peter promptly, and backed away in a rather undignified manner. Just looking at that cold, black water made him chilly.

"Oh, come on, Peter! It is the greatest fun in the world!" cried Little Joe, and giving a quick, hard push with his hind feet he glided right down that furrow flat on his stomach straight into the water. Peter looked over at the trail Little Joe had made getting up there. Then in a flash he understood. That trail which had puzzled him so was made by Little Joe Otter himself. He had made those queer furrows by sliding on his stomach in the same way that he had gone down that bank. Peter gave a happy little sigh. His curiosity was satisfied.

CHAPTER XIV

THE COASTING PARTY

Who fun in life himself denies
Becomes a grouch before he dies.

Little Joe Otter.

PETER RABBIT was so tickled over having discovered who made the queer trail in the snow that he quite forgot to look down in the Laughing Brook to see where Little Joe Otter went to. When he did think to look, Little Joe was nowhere to be seen. Peter waited awhile, hoping that Little Joe would return. He wanted to see him slide down that bank again.

At last Peter decided that Little Joe had gone home, and that there was no use sitting on the snow-covered bank of the Laughing Brook any longer. He was just turning away when he heard a splash from the Laughing Brook. He stopped to look up stream. At once he saw four swimmers coming down the Laughing Brook and appearing to have no end of fun as they rolled over in the water, dived, swam under water, and moved swiftly along, with just their heads showing. They were Little Joe Otter, Mrs. Otter, and their two nearly grown children.

When they reached the place where Peter had first seen Little Joe climb out and up the bank,

Little Joe made straight for shore. You remember that the bank was low there. Out he scrambled. Out behind him scrambled Mrs. Otter. Out behind her scrambled one of the young Otters, and out behind this one scrambled the other young Otter. Then, following the trail Little Joe had made in the snow, they came straight up along the bank towards where Peter was sitting. Peter suddenly felt bashful. He retreated rather hurriedly to the shelter of a snow-covered hemlock bough. He could n't help a suspicion that one of those Otters might suddenly think that a Rabbit dinner would taste good.

Little Joe led the way to the edge of the steep bank where

Peter had watched him slide down. With a quick, hard kick of his hind feet he disappeared down that bank and a second later Peter heard a splash in the water. Then Mrs. Otter did the same thing, and the two young Otters followed. Peter remained right where he was. In a few minutes he saw Little Joe Otter coming back up the trail again. And behind him came Mrs. Otter and the two young Otters. "I do believe they're going to slide again," thought Peter. "I must get where I can watch them."

So Peter crept out of his hiding-place and over to the edge of the bank, where from a safe distance he could watch Little Joe and his family.   Again, flat on his stomach, Little Joe came sliding down that furrow in the snow straight into the Laughing Brook. One of the young Otters could n't wait for Mrs. Otter to go down in that same furrow and made a furrow of his own.   The other followed right at his heels.   Then there was a great swimming race to see who could get back to the low place on the bank first, and then another race through the snow to get to the top of the slide.

Such a merry coasting party as that was.   Every time one of those Otters disappeared in the black, cold-looking water, Peter shivered. He just could n't help it.   But there was no shivering on the part

of Little Joe and his family. Not
a bit of it! They appeared to
enjoy those plunges into the water
quite as much as they would have
had it been a midsummer day. The
more they slid the better the slide
became and the faster they went.

"Come on and join us, Peter!"
cried Little Joe, as he kicked off
and went shooting down.

Peter shook his head. He did
it a little wistfully. Those Otters
were having such a merry time
that Peter envied them. But every
time he looked at that water, so
cold and black, he shivered. The
coasting part might be all right,
but Peter preferred to try it where
there was no water at the end of
the slide.

GENTLE MISTRESS MOON SAW A QUEER PROCESSION.
Page 95.

CHAPTER XV

LITTLE JOE AND MRS. JOE REACH A DECISION

To eager youth 'tis vain to preach;
Experience alone can teach.

Little Joe Otter.

Rough Brother North Wind and Jack Frost had been down from the Far North for some time now. The pond of Paddy the Beaver, the Smiling Pool, and the Laughing Brook, excepting where it ran swiftly, were covered with ice. The Green Meadows and the Green Forest and the Old Pasture were deep with snow. Only those who, like Johnny Chuck and

Nimble Heels the Jumping Mouse and Striped Chipmunk and Bobby Coon, were asleep in their snug homes, or, like Paddy the Beaver and Jerry Muskrat, had plenty to eat close by their houses, had nothing to worry about. Those who had to hunt for their food were having a hard time of it. They always do in winter.

Little Joe Otter and his family had cause for worry. You know they live on fish. But now they were having to work as they never had before to get enough to eat. You see, they had been fishing so long in the Smiling Pool and along the Laughing Brook that fish were becoming scarce. It was the morning after the coasting party that Little Joe and Mrs. Otter went without breakfast that the two young Otters might eat.

"My dear," said Little Joe, "this is the poorest fishing I have ever known. So much of the Laughing Brook is frozen over that only a few places are left in which we can fish. And we have already caught most of the fish in those places. We have got to do something about it."

"I've been thinking that very thing," replied Mrs. Otter. "Shall we take the youngsters down to the Big River?"

"I know of another brook, a bigger brook than this, which has deep spring holes in it, and many places where the water is swift and does not freeze. We might go there first," said Little Joe.

"Is it far from here?" asked Mrs. Otter.

Little Joe admitted that it was very far from there. "But what of it?" said he. "It will give the youngsters a chance to see something of the Great World, and that will be good for them. When we reach that brook we can stay there as long as there is good fishing, and then follow it down to the Big River. Then we can come down the Big River and so back here to the Laughing Brook."

Mrs. Otter thought this over for a few minutes. "Wouldn't such a journey over land be dangerous?" she asked.

"Are you afraid?" asked Little Joe.

"Not for myself," snapped Mrs. Otter rather sharply. "It is the children I am thinking of."

"They've never been in any real danger," said Little Joe. "It would be a good thing for them to make a journey on which they must watch out all the time. It would teach them how to take care of themselves."

Mrs. Otter scratched her nose thoughtfully. "When do we start?" she asked very suddenly.

"To-night," replied Little Joe promptly. "It will be moonlight to-night. Besides, the sooner we start, the sooner we'll get a good meal."

"You're sure you know the way?" asked Mrs. Otter a bit doubtfully.

"Of course," replied Little Joe. "Do you think I would propose going if I did n't know the way?"

So it was decided that the Otter family would start on a journey that very night.

CHAPTER XVI

THE FUN OF TRAVELING

Who travels much will wiser be,
Provided he has eyes to see.

Little Joe Otter.

GENTLE Mistress Moon, peeping down though the tops of the trees of the Green Forest, saw a queer procession going up the Laughing Brook to the pond of Paddy the Beaver, deep in the Green Forest. They were Little Joe Otter, Mrs. Otter, and the two nearly grown young Otters. Little Joe was leading, the others following in single file.

When they reached the pond of Paddy the Beaver they found it covered with smooth ice. The snow had fallen before the pond had frozen over. Little Joe made three or four jumps and then threw himself flat on his stomach and away he slid on the smooth ice. As soon as he stopped sliding he scrambled to his feet and did the same thing again. The others did just as he did. They squealed with delight. It was great fun. And it was surprising how fast they went across the pond of Paddy the Beaver. When they got to the other side the young Otters did n't want to leave that pond. They wanted to slide some more.

But they had been well brought

up, and when Little Joe promised
them that they should have more
sliding before they reached the
end of their journey they said
nothing more. Into the woods,
plowing through the snow, Little
Joe led the way. Every time there
was a little slope he would slide
down to the bottom. Of course
all the others did the same. Sometimes where it was level he would
make a few swift jumps and then
slide on his stomach.

The young Otters were much
excited. It was the first time they
had been any distance from the
Laughing Brook. Everything was
strange and new and wonderful.
They wanted to stop to examine
everything. They startled Jumper

the Hare, and as he bounded away
the young Otters started after him
and could n't understand why Little
Joe and Mrs. Otter called them
back. Mrs. Grouse whirred out
from under a low hemlock tree and
gave them a great fright. Both
jumped at the roar of those stout
wings. Then, as they saw that
their father and mother had n't
even turned their heads, they
looked a little ashamed.

Little Joe Otter chose the easiest
way. If he could slip under a
log instead of climbing over it,
he did so. When he could n't slip
under it he went around it. But
though he made a trail that was
very winding, he always kept to
a certain direction. It was clear

that he knew exactly where he was heading for.

Now Otters have short legs, and traveling in the soft snow was tiresome, even though they could slide now and then. So at last the two young Otters began to lag a little. Traveling was becoming more work than fun. Little Joe knew just how they felt. He had n't forgotten his first journey when he was a youngster. So when at last he came to a great upturned tree, he dived into the snow and disappeared. In a moment he poked his head out of the hole he had made.

"We 'll stop here for a rest," said he, and once more disappeared.

Mrs. Otter and the two young

Otters followed him. They found him in the snuggest, warmest little cave under the roots of that old tree. It was just the place to rest and sleep. In two minutes those young Otters were curled up and sound asleep. Little Joe and Mrs. Otter talked for a few minutes, and then they, too, curled up.

CHAPTER XVII

YOWLER THE BOBCAT FOLLOWS

The opportunist oft succeeds
Because of trifles that he heeds.

Little Joe Otter.

YOWLER the Bobcat, prowling about through the Green Forest, came across the trail of the Otter family. He did n't have to use his nose to follow that trail. Any one with eyes could follow it. The instant he saw it Yowler knew who had made that trail.

"Huh!" muttered Yowler. "Little Joe Otter has started on his travels again. I wonder where he is going this time."

Then Yowler, more from habit than anything else, put his nose down in that trail and sniffed. A surprising change came over him. He suddenly took great interest in that trail. He had smelled *young* Otters. Little Joe or Mrs. Otter he wouldn't think of attacking. They were too big and strong, and he knew too well how they could fight. But a young Otter would be a different matter, even though he might be almost fully grown. Certainly this was a matter worth looking into.

So in his usual, sneaking fashion Yowler followed that trail. And at length he came to the big up-turned tree and the hole in the snow that led down under the roots.

Very gently Yowler sniffed. At once his nose was filled with the Otter scent. He grinned hungrily. Those Otters were down there asleep. It was a great temptation to dig down and try to surprise them. But Yowler knew better than to try this. He looked around. A short distance away was a big hemlock tree. Yowler circled around to it and climbed part way up. Then he crouched on a big limb and prepared to wait for those Otters to come out.

He didn't have long to wait. He saw the head of Little Joe Otter pop out of that hole in the snow. Then Little Joe came out. He was followed by Mrs. Otter and then by the two young Otters.

Yowler's yellow eyes glowed hungrily as he noticed that one of these was smaller than the other.

Little Joe started off at once, and the others fell in behind him. Just as soon as he dared to, Yowler dropped down from that tree and began to sneak after them. It was surprising how fast those Otters traveled. But Yowler can travel fast, and it was n't long before he had them in sight. Then he moved more cautiously. He sneaked from tree to tree and took advantage of every stump and bush. For awhile the young Otters kept close to their parents. Then from time to time they dropped back, as they stopped to examine things that were new to them. Their curiosity satisfied, they would bound ahead to catch up.

"If that smallest Otter will just drop far enough behind so that I can get her alone, I think I'll have an Otter dinner," muttered Yowler. "Those youngsters have got to see everything that is to be seen. They are like all other youngsters, full of curiosity and heedless. They probably think they are quite able to take care of themselves. It certainly will be worth while to follow them for awhile. I haven't anything better to do. Besides, I will go a long way for an Otter dinner." He licked his lips and his mouth watered.

CHAPTER XVIII

THE SMALLEST OTTER IS WILFUL

The wilful and the heedless gain
Experience through fright and pain.

Little Joe Otter.

LITTLE JOE and Mrs. Otter are wise in the ways and the things of the Green Forest. So, as they journeyed towards the distant brook they had planned to visit, their keen ears caught every little sound, and without bothering to investigate they knew just what had made each little sound. But with the two young Otters it was a very different matter. Everything was new and strange and therefore interesting. They wanted to stop and examine everything. Every time they heard a little noise off at one side they wanted to go over and find out what had made it.

Now Mrs. Otter is a good mother, a watchful mother. She kept a keen eye on the two young Otters. And every time they started off she called them back. She warned them that there were dangers in the Green Forest. She did her best to frighten them.

The smallest Otter was head-strong and wilful and heedless. She wanted to have her own way. "Mother is just trying to scare us," she whispered to her brother.

"I don't believe there is any danger. We haven't seen a single thing to be afraid of. She wants us to tag along at her heels and not have any fun. I want to see all there is to see. She can't scare me. I'm not afraid of any one."

So the smallest Otter kept dropping behind to examine everything that interested her. At the same time she kept a watchful eye on Mrs. Otter, and every time the latter turned to see where the youngsters were, the smallest Otter would go bounding along the trail, hurrying to catch up.

Her brother was more obedient. He sometimes dropped behind, but never as far behind as his sister. Mother Otter, seeing the obedient young Otter not far behind, would take it for granted that his sister was not far behind him, and so after a while she became a little less watchful. The smallest Otter soon discovered this, and then she dropped farther back than ever.

"I can't get lost," said she to herself, "because all I have to do is to follow this trail through the snow. I don't care if they do get way ahead. I can catch up any time by hurrying. Now I wonder what that is. I am sure I saw something move under that little tree over to the right."

She stopped and looked very hard at the young tree. The branches were bent down with snow. She could n't see under them. There was nothing moving there now. She looked up the trail. Little Joe and Mrs. Otter were out of sight, and her brother was just disappearing over the top of a little ridge.

"I'm sure I saw something move over there," said the wilful young Otter, looking back at the little tree. "I'm sure I did. It won't take but a minute to go over and find out. Mother always has said that we should learn all we can. How can we learn if we don't try to find out about things? There certainly won't be any harm in looking under that little tree."

Once more she glanced along the trail. Her brother had disappeared. No one was in sight. Then she turned and bounded through the snow towards that little hemlock tree. She was going to satisfy her curiosity.

CHAPTER XIX

THE YOUNG OTTER'S CURIOSITY IS SATISFIED

True courage ne'er gives way to fear
When unexpected foes appear.

Little Joe Otter.

NEVER was Peter Rabbit more filled with curiosity than was the wilful little Otter plunging through the snow towards a certain little snow-covered tree. She was sure that she had seen something move under that little tree. She had n't the least bit of fear. Never in her short life had she been in real danger. Never had she had a real fright. You see always her father, Little Joe Otter, or her mother, had been close at hand. And of course, with father or mother near, there was never anything to be afraid of.

Now the lowest boughs of that little hemlock tree were bent to the ground by the snow on them. Under them it was dark. It was in this darkness that the little Otter had thought she saw something move. She kept her bright eyes fixed on it as she drew nearer. A few feet from it she stopped abruptly. In that darkness under the boughs of the little tree were two little spots of light. The young Otter stared and blinked and stared again. Gradually she made out a face. The two little

spots of light were two eyes, glow-
ing with hunger and savage eagerness. The face was a fierce-looking face. Never had the young
Otter seen such a fierce-looking
face. For the first time in her life
a chill of fear ran all over her.

She no longer had any curiosity.
Whose face it was she was staring
at she had n't the least idea. She
did n't even want to find out.
She suddenly wished she was back
where she should have been with
her father and mother and brother.
She turned and bounded back towards the trail. The instant she
turned a yellowish-brown form
bounded out from beneath the
young tree. It was Yowler the
Bobcat.

Despite the shortness of her legs, the young Otter moved fast. But with his longer legs Yowler moved faster. By the time she was back on the trail Yowler was only a jump behind her. Never was there a more frightened youngster in all the Great World than was that young Otter. But she was no coward. Like a flash she turned to face Yowler, spitting and snarling.

For an instant Yowler hesitated. He had hoped to spring on her back, but he hadn't been quite quick enough. She was now nearly grown, and she was big enough to fight hard. So Yowler hesitated. But it was only for a moment. He knew that she was young and probably never had been in a fight. He was quite willing to be bitten and scratched a little for the sake of such a dinner as that young Otter would make him. So with a snarl Yowler sprang at her.

He tried to seize her by the throat, but she was too quick for him. The next instant they were rolling over and over in the snow, snarling, spitting, growling, biting and clawing at each other. Now Yowler likes to fight on his back, so that he can use those great, stout hind feet of his to rip and tear. But an Otter, like other members of the Weasel family, can twist and turn in a marvelous way. So the young

Otter managed to keep out of reach of those clawing hind feet.

Such a fight as that was! There was no longer any fear in that young Otter. She was simply fighting mad. But Yowler was bigger and stronger, and he was an old fighter. It certainly looked bad for that wilful, heedless, young Otter.

CHAPTER XX

A VERY MEEK YOUNG OTTER

*The wise will never scorn retreat
When facing swift and sure defeat.*

Little Joe Otter.

Yes, Sir, it certainly looked bad for that young Otter fighting with Yowler the Bobcat. It looked very much as if in the end Yowler would have that dinner of tender, young Otter for which he was fighting. Such a snarling and spitting! Such a thrashing about in the snow, as they rolled over and over! Never had Yowler fought harder.

But though he was so busy with teeth and claws, he never once forgot to keep his ears open. He never once forgot to listen for sounds that might warn him of the approach of Little Joe Otter or Mrs. Joe. He knew that they were not so far away but that they might hear that fight. So it was with a sudden wrench he tore himself free, and with a screech of disappointment and anger bounded to the nearest tree and climbed it.

He was just in time and that was all. Snarling, her eyes blazing with anger, Mrs. Joe plunged down the trail, and behind her came Little Joe Otter. Had they succeeded in reaching Yowler, the

Green Forest would have known him no more.

Mrs. Joe paid no attention to him. She rushed straight to the young Otter and began to lick her wounds and try to comfort her. She examined her all over to see how badly she was hurt, as only an anxious mother could. But Little Joe made straight for the tree up which Yowler had climbed. At the foot of it he glared up and dared Yowler to come down. Yowler was licking a badly bitten paw. Between licks he snarled and growled and spit at Little Joe. But he did n't come down. No, Sir, Yowler did n't come down. He was far too wise to do that. And so all that Little Joe could do was to snarl and spit back at him and tell him what he would do to him if ever he had the chance.

It didn't take Mrs. Joe long to find that the young Otter was not badly hurt. Her coat was torn in places and she was very, very sore, but she was not seriously hurt. As soon as Mrs. Joe was sure of this she called to Little Joe, and regretfully Little Joe left the foot of that tree and once more led the way along the trail. This time Mrs. Joe was the last one. She kept behind the two young Otters. She didn't intend to give them a chance to get into more trouble.

As for the young Otter, never

was there one more meek. She had
had a lesson she would never forget. She smarted and ached, but
she knew that she deserved it.
She knew that it was wholly because of her wilfulness and dis-
obedience.

"I 'll never, never disobey again,"
she kept saying over and over to
herself. " I 'll never, never disobey
again. I guess I don't know as
much about the Great World as I
thought I did. Ouch! That fellow's teeth and claws were sharp.
I — I — I wish I had n't thought
myself so smart. I wonder who
that fellow is, anyway."

Before this she had been too
busy to even wonder who she had
been fighting with. But now she

wanted to know who this enemy was. And so at the first chance she asked her mother.

"That was Yowler the Bobcat," replied her mother. "He is the greatest sneak in the Green Forest. He wouldn't have dared to touch your father or me. I wish we had been in time to catch him. There are a lot of people who would have been thankful to us if we had."

CHAPTER XXI

A RACE FOR LIFE

When life's at stake 'tis no disgrace
To run from what you dare not face.
Little Joe Otter.

LITTLE Joe Otter and his family
had traveled many miles from the
Laughing Brook on their way to
that other brook where Little Joe
was sure they would find better
fishing. They had left a deep trail
through the snow. It happened
that this trail was found by an old
trapper, who was tramping through
the woods.

"Traveling Otter!" he exclaimed, as soon as he saw that trail. Then he examined the trail very carefully. "More than one has been along here," he decided. "What is more, those Otters are not very far ahead of me. This trail is very fresh. They're heading straight for the pond just beyond the next ridge. Otter fur brings high prices these days. If I can catch up with them, I may be able to get a skin or two."

He looked around for a stout club, and as soon as he had found one to suit him he hurried along that trail. He guessed that those Otters were not hurrying. He hoped that if he could get near enough before he was discovered, he would be able to outrun one or two of them. So he hurried on as fast as he could, taking the greatest care to make as little noise as possible.

Little Joe, Mrs. Joe and the two young Otters had almost reached the pond when Little Joe's ears caught a sound that caused him to stop and look back along their trail. He saw that man running. He recognized him instantly as one of those two-legged creatures called men, the only enemies Little Joe really feared. "We must run for our lives!" he cried and led the way, breaking the path through the snow.

Then began a race for life. Little Joe knew that if that man caught up with them, they would have no chance for their lives. He knew all about that pond just ahead. He knew that at one end there were springs and that when all the rest of the pond was covered with ice, there usually was open water above those springs. If they could reach open water they would be safe.

Such a race as that was! Though the Otters did their best, they could not travel as fast through the snow as the man. He gained on them with every step. How thankful Little Joe and Mrs. Joe were that he had no terrible gun. Had he carried a terrible gun they would have had no chance at all. But even without a terrible gun he would surely kill them all unless they could reach that open water.

Through the trees they saw the black, smooth ice of that pond just ahead of them. They bounded and plunged ahead with all their strength. Little Joe was ahead to break the way through the snow. Then came the two young Otters, and Mrs. Joe was last. That trapper was almost within striking distance as she sprang out on to the ice. Out there the Otters could travel faster than the trapper. They would make several bounds forward and then throw themselves on their stomachs and slide. It was surprising how fast they traveled over that ice. But the trapper couldn't run fast on the ice. It was too slippery. He did his best, but he fell farther and farther be-

hind. Finally he threw his club
at Mrs. Joe. It just missed her.
A minute later, one after another,
Little Joe and his family disappeared in the open water. They
had won their race for life.

CHAPTER XXII

THE CLEVER TRAPPER

The trapper knows his wits must match
The wits of those whom he would catch.
Little Joe Otter.

THE trapper who had tried to
run down Little Joe Otter and his
family and kill them with a club
was not one to give up easily. Of
course, he was disappointed at his
failure to get one of those Otter
coats. But he was not at all discouraged. As soon as Little Joe
Otter and his family had disappeared in the open water at one

end of that pond, the trapper stopped running. He was glad to stop, for he was quite out of breath.

"Those Otters won't stay in this pond long," said he to himself. "They know that I know they are here, so they will move on as soon as they think they safely can. I can guess just where they are bound for. They are bound for the big brook where there is a lot of swift water that does n't freeze, and where they will be sure of good fishing. They will stay there for some time. That will be the place to set some traps. The thing for me to do is to leave them alone for awhile so that they will not be at all suspicious. Then

I'll set some traps. Their fur is in the best of condition now, and if I can get two or three of their skins they will pay me several times over for all the trouble I may take to get them."

So the trapper turned back and tramped home. He didn't go back to that pond for two days. When he did go back he found just what he expected to find, and he chuckled when he found it. It was a trail in the snow leading away from that pond in the direction of the big brook. He followed it. As he approached the big brook he was careful to keep out of sight. He could see that the trail led straight to the water. For a long time he remained hid-

den, patiently watching. At last
he saw a brown head out in the
water. A moment later one of
the young Otters with a fish in his
mouth climbed out on a big, flat
rock and ate the fish.

"They are there," chuckled the
trapper, "and they will stay, for
there are plenty of fish there. I
won't worry them for awhile, but I
will study their habits and find out
where they are in the habit of going and what their favorite places
are. They will be sure to have a
slide. That will be one place for
a trap. I'll put it right at the
foot of the slide. I'll find out
where they are in the habit of
climbing out on the bank to go up
to the top of the slide and I'll put

a trap there. Perhaps I can discover the den where they sleep.
That will be another place for a
trap. I suspect that those old
Otters (he meant Little Joe and
Mrs. Joe) have learned a lot about
traps, and it will not be easy to
catch them. But I ought to be
able to catch those two young Otters without much trouble."

So for a week that trapper
spent most of his time watching
the place where Little Joe and his
family were living, and studying
the signs to learn all he could
about their habits. But all the
time he took the greatest care that
they should n't know he was about.
He knew that if he should be seen
by one of them, Little Joe Otter

would at once become suspicious.
When at last he felt he had learned
all he could he selected a dozen
cruel, steel traps and went over to
set them.

CHAPTER XXIII

THE SETTING OF THE TRAPS

There's always some one setting traps
While honest folk are taking naps.

Little Joe Otter.

THE trapper had found out the things he wanted to know. He had found out where the Otters left the water to climb up to the top of their slippery slide. He had found out where they were in the habit of making a short cut across from one part of the brook to another where it made a bend. He had found certain favorite places where they brought the fish they had caught to eat. He felt that the time now had come to set traps.

Now this trapper knew that an Otter has a keen nose and is very suspicious. He knew that if he handled those traps with his bare hands, Little Joe or Mrs. Joe would be likely to get the dreaded man smell and would keep away from those traps. So he took care not to touch them with bare hands.

He first took great care to make sure that none of the Otter family were about. Then he set those cruel traps. One he placed in the water right at the foot of the bank where the Otters were in the habit of climbing out to go up to their slippery slide. He placed it in such a way that the first Otter who tried to climb up that bank would be sure to step in the trap.

In the short cut that Little Joe and his family had made so as not to have to go way around the bend he placed two traps, one at each end of the little path. He covered them lightly with snow so that they could not be seen. Other traps were hidden in a similar way at places he knew the Otters often visited. One trap was set right at the foot of the slippery slide. There was no bait with any of these traps. In another part of the brook, which he knew the Otters visited occasionally to fish, traps were set, each baited with a fish.

"There," said the trapper, when the last trap had been set, "if those Otters manage to keep out of all those traps they will prove themselves to be smarter than I think they are. This is the first day of the new year, and unless I am greatly mistaken, one or more of those Otters will have a New Year surprise party."

Then the trapper hurried away. He had worked fast, for he didn't want to be seen. He knew that if Little Joe or Mrs. Joe should see him, they would at once become suspicious. He was sure that he hadn't been seen, and all the way home he chuckled as he thought of how clever and smart he had been. He didn't once think of how dreadful it would be for one of those little people in brown fur to be caught in one of those cruel traps. All he thought about was the money that one of those brown fur coats would bring him.

While the trapper had been so busy setting those traps, Little Joe Otter, Mrs. Joe, and the two young Otters had been taking a nap. They knew nothing of the trapper's visit to the brook. They were care-free and happy and life was very good to them.

CHAPTER XXIV

LITTLE JOE OTTER IS SUSPICIOUS

Suspicious folk avoid mishaps
By always watching out for traps.
Little Joe Otter.

HARDLY had the trapper disappeared in the woods when Little Joe Otter awoke and crept forth from his hiding-place. He left Mrs. Otter and the two young Otters still asleep. Little Joe yawned, stretched, and then decided that he wanted a trout. It didn't take him long to catch one. With it in his mouth he swam straight to a certain old log, one end of which was in the water. He intended to climb out on that old log and eat that trout. It was his favorite eating place.

But just as he reached that old log and before he had started to climb out on it, a queer feeling of uneasiness took possession of him. He had a feeling that something wasn't quite right. Now when Little Joe has that feeling he always heeds it. He didn't climb out on that log. He turned and swam over to a flat rock. He climbed out on that and laid the fish down. Somehow he had lost his appetite. He looked long and hard over at that old log.

"It looks all right," said Little Joe. "Yes, Sir, it looks all right.

Just the same I have a feeling that there is something wrong there. I believe I'll go back there and see if I can find out what *is* wrong."

So once more Little Joe swam to that old log. But he did n't climb out on it. He studied it and studied it. He used both eyes and nose. Presently he noticed some fresh mud on that old log. That was queer. He was sure there had been no mud there before. Very carefully he looked all around the place where that fresh mud was, and in doing this he discovered a chain. He got hold of the chain and pulled gently. What do you think happened? Why, he pulled a trap up out of a place that had been cut in that old log, and then covered with mud to hide the freshly cut wood.

"Ha!" exclaimed Little Joe, as the trap dropped down into the water beside the old log. "I've been afraid of this ever since we were chased by that terrible two-legged creature on our way over here. He must be the one who set this trap. If he set this trap, he has set other traps. I must warn Mrs. Joe and the children. That trapper has been watching us. He knows that I have been using this old log. He probably knows all the other places where we are in the habit of going. We must find out where those traps are."

Just then Little Joe heard a splash in the water. There was Mrs. Joe with a trout in her mouth. He called her over there, and showed her the trap and where it had been set. "Where are the children?" he demanded.

"They are fishing," replied Mrs. Otter, with a most anxious look in her eyes. "We must find them at once. They never have seen a trap and they know nothing about traps. Oh, dear, I hope they will not get caught before we can find them and warn them!"

Just then the smallest young Otter climbed out on a rock, and a moment later her brother climbed out on another rock. Mrs. Otter and Little Joe swam swiftly over to them. The young Otters stopped eating the fish they had caught to stare in surprise at the way in which their parents were hurrying.

CHAPTER XXV

THE YOUNG OTTERS ARE WARNED

The young who heed an elder's warning
Show evidence of wisdom's dawning.

Little Joe Otter.

"Do you remember the terrible two-legged creature who chased us on our way from the Laughing Brook to this brook?" Little Joe Otter asked the two young Otters.

Both nodded their heads. "I guess I do!" exclaimed one. "He gave me a dreadful fright."

"Have you seen anything of him since we have been staying over here?" Mrs. Joe asked.

This time both the young Otters shook their heads. "No," said the one who had spoken before. "The truth is, I had forgotten all about him. I guess he does n't know we are over here."

"I guess he does," said Little Joe Otter. "I *know* he does. He has set traps for us."

"What are traps?" asked one of the young Otters.

"They are terrible things with awful jaws which are hidden where they are not likely to be seen and are always ready to jump up and seize an Otter by the leg. Then they will never let go, and there is no way of making them let go," explained Little Joe.

The eyes of the young Otters

grew round with wonder and fear. "But what have they to do with that terrible creature who chased us?" asked one of them.

"Those traps belong to him," replied Little Joe. "He is the one who has hidden those traps, hoping to catch us. If one of you should be caught in one of those traps, that terrible two-legged creature would come and kill you."

"But how do you know that he has hidden any of those dreadful traps around here?" inquired the smallest Otter.

"Your father has just found one," replied Mrs. Joe. "It was set over on that old log where your father has been in the habit of eating his fish. Probably there are more traps, and so it is not going to be safe for any of us to go to the places we have been in the habit of going. That means that you must not use the slippery slide again, not even once. You must keep away from the bank at the place where we have been in the habit of climbing it to reach the top of the slippery slide. Each of you must promise not to once use that little path we have made across the point to reach that other bend in the brook."

"But can't we slide any more?" asked one young Otter, looking very much disappointed. "There won't be any fun if we can't go sliding."

"It is better to go without fun

than to lose your life," said Little Joe Otter gravely. "However, we will make a new slippery slide. There is one thing more: If one of you should find a dead fish, keep away from it."

"Why?" demanded one of the young Otters.

"Because the only safe fish for an Otter is a live fish. No matter how hungry you are or how hard it is to catch a fish, don't be tempted by a dead fish. There is likely to be a trap hidden close by. If the fishing were not so good here, we would move on at once. Now remember to keep away from every place you have been in the habit of going to, and don't touch a dead fish."

CHAPTER XXVI

THE FOOLISH YOUNG OTTER

Youth too often scorns advice
And in the end must pay the price.

Little Joe Otter.

LITTLE Joe Otter took the two
young Otters over to the log where
he had found the trap and showed
it to them. It looked so harmless
that it was difficult for the young
Otters to believe that it was such
a terrible thing as their father said
it was. Then he took them over
to the foot of the slippery slide,
and while they swam about at a
safe distance he looked carefully

until he found a trap right at the bottom of the slippery slide. He showed it to them.

"Now you see why I said you must n't go down the slippery slide even once," said he. "I did n't know that this trap was here, but I suspected it. I suspect that there are traps in the other places I have warned you to keep away from. If you want to live long and be happy, don't once forget the warnings your mother and I have given you."

The young Otters promised they would n't forget, and then the whole family went fishing. Of course, they did n't go fishing together. They separated, each one fishing in a different place. All the time she was looking for a trout, the smallest Otter kept thinking about those traps. She made up her mind that nothing would tempt her to be heedless of the warnings she had been given. You see, she had not forgotten the lesson she had learned when Yowler the Bobcat had caught her because of her heedless wilfulness.

But her brother had had no such lesson, and as he hunted for trout he smiled to himself at what he thought were the foolish fears of his parents. "Father and mother are just trying to scare us," said he. "I don't believe there is anything to be afraid of as long as that dreadful two-legged creature is n't about. Those traps look perfectly harmless to me. I'm not afraid of them. I guess if I use my eyes and my nose I can find them without getting into one of them. I wonder where all the fish have gone to. My, I'm hungry! I believe I'll go farther up the brook. There is some swift, open water up there and it hasn't been fished much."

So the young Otter swam to the upper end of the open water where he then was, climbed out on the ice and traveled over this until he came to another stretch of open water. He swam along close to the bank on one side and presently came to a sort of little pen of sticks. He didn't remember having seen it before, and he looked at it suspiciously. He swam around it at a safe distance, and then he smelled fish. It did n't take him long to discover that inside of that little pen, at the back, was a fat trout. That trout was n't alive. It seemed to be held by a stick at the back of that little pen.

The young Otter remembered the warning not to touch a dead fish. But he was hungry, very hungry, and here was a dinner he would n't have to take the trouble to catch. He swam back and forth in front of that little pen of sticks and examined them carefully. He went close to them and smelled of them. They seemed nothing but harmless sticks. His mouth began to water at the smell of the fish.

"There isn't a particle of danger," said the foolish young Otter. "There wouldn't be a trap way up here, anyway. I want that fish and I'm going to have it."

CHAPTER XXVII

A SUDDENLY LOST APPETITE

By pain and fright is wisdom bought,
And thus respect for elders taught.

Little Joe Otter.

LITTLE Joe Otter's foolish young
son, who had found a dead fish at
the back of a little pen of sticks
on the edge of the water, remembered the warning to leave dead
fish alone. But he was hungry,
and it would n't take but a second
to get that fish.

"Father and mother were just
trying to scare us," he repeated
to himself. "I guess they don't
realize that I am big enough to

take care of myself. It won't be long before I will be leaving them and going out into the Great World for myself, anyway. Then I'll have to depend on my own judgment. This fish is just waiting for me. I don't know how it happened to get here, but that doesn't make any difference. I would be a silly fellow to waste my time hunting for a live fish when a dead one is waiting for me right under my nose."

So with a look all around to make sure that no one was watching him, the foolish young Otter entered the little pen of sticks through a narrow opening, his eyes shining as he reached for the dead fish at the back of the pen.

And then something happened! Yes, indeed, something happened! Something grabbed the foolish young Otter by one of his toes! Yes, Sir, it grabbed him and it grabbed him tight! What it was he had n't the least idea. But whatever it was, it hurt dreadfully.

And the young Otter suffered more from fright than he did from pain. He twisted around and plunged for the deep water, but he was brought up short. The thing that had grabbed him by the toe was holding on. He struggled, but he was held fast. The dreadful thing was pulling him down under water. If it should succeed in holding him down there he would drown. My, how he did thrash about and struggle! Even yet he did n't know what it was that was holding him.

By and by he had to stop struggling in order to get his breath. His foot ached dreadfully. Without really thinking of what he was doing, he swam towards the shore. Then he found that this thing that had him by the toe did n't pull him under water. He twisted around to see what it was that was holding him. It was a cruel, steel trap. He knew what it was as soon as he saw it, for his father, Little Joe Otter, had shown him one that very morning.

Right within reach was that fish which had been the cause of all this trouble. The young Otter did n't even look at it. He, who had been so hungry a few minutes before, had lost his appetite. Yes, Sir, he had lost his appetite completely. Just then he felt as if he did n't care ever to eat again.

All he wanted was to get away from that dreadful trap. He bit at it, but this only hurt his teeth. It held him as tightly as ever. He remembered what Little Joe Otter had told him, about how if he should be caught in a trap that dreadful two-legged creature would come and kill him. Once more he began to struggle. He pulled with all his might. It hurt, but he kept on pulling. But for all his pulling he was held fast.

CHAPTER XXVIII

THE PRICE OF FREEDOM

For freedom who is there will say
There's any price too much to pay?
                                    Little Joe Otter.

HAVE you ever been terribly frightened? Have you ever been so frightened that you couldn't even think? That is the way it was with the foolish young Otter when he realized that he was caught in a trap. He was so filled with terror that he didn't even think about the pain in his foot. There is nothing quite so awful as the helpless feeling that comes when one is caught in a trap. Had that young Otter been seized by an enemy twice his size he would have fought bravely to the last breath. But one cannot fight a steel trap.

After awhile the young Otter was so tired out with struggling that he had to be quiet to get his breath and to rest. He trembled all over. Every time he heard the least little sound he was sure it was the trapper coming to kill him. How he did wish he had heeded the warnings of his father and mother !

For a long, long, long time he was held a prisoner by that dreadful trap. From time to time he tried to cut the chain that held the trap, but of course he tried in vain. His teeth, sharp as they were, did n't even scratch the steel of that chain. He wondered if his father and mother would miss him and look for him. He wondered if they would ever find out what had happened to him.

"If I could only get away from this thing, I never, never would disobey again," he sobbed. "No, Sir, I never, *never* would disobey again. I do wish father and mother would come. Perhaps if they came they could get me free from this dreadful thing."

It is said that if you wish long enough and hard enough for a thing you may get your wish. Certainly the foolish young Otter wished long and hard. And at last he did get his wish. His father, Little Joe Otter, suddenly appeared. He was looking for that young Otter. He had worried when that young Otter did not return and had started out to look for him.

Little Joe didn't scold that young Otter. Instead, he did the best he could to comfort him. The first thing he did was to look to see how the young Otter was held by that dreadful trap. He saw right away that he was held only by one toe.

"You are lucky, very lucky," declared Little Joe Otter.

The young Otter thought he was very unlucky. He said so. He couldn't see that there was anything lucky about it. Then Little Joe explained.

"That trap," said he, "has got you only by one toe. It might have you by the whole foot. If it had you by the whole foot, and that is the way the trapper meant that it should catch you, there would be very little hope for you. As it is, if you pull hard enough, you may lose your toe, but that will be all."

"But I don't want to lose my toe!" wailed the young Otter.

"All right," replied Little Joe. "If you had rather lose your life than your toe, there is nothing I can do about it. You can get free if you really want to, but the price of freedom will be that toe."

CHAPTER XXIX

THE YOUNG OTTER PAYS THE PRICE

If life and freedom be the cost,
What matter if a toe is lost?

Little Joe Otter.

HAVE you ever tried to make
up your mind to have an aching
tooth pulled? If you have, you
remember what hard work it was
and how you kept putting it off
and putting it off and putting it
off. It was the same way with
the young Otter caught in a steel
trap by one toe. His father,
Little Joe Otter, had told him that
there was only one way in which

he could gain freedom, and that was by losing that toe. He had told him that he would have to lose that toe or lose his life.

But the young Otter did n't want to lose his toe. He said so over and over. He just could n't make up his mind to it. It seemed to him a dreadful thing to lose a toe.

"What is losing your toe compared with losing your life?" his father asked.

"But perhaps I won't lose my life," protested the young Otter.

"Yes, you will," replied Little Joe Otter. "It is just as certain as it is that you are now caught in this trap. I can't help you; your mother can't help you; no one can help you. That two-legged creature who set this dreadful trap will come to see if any one has been caught in it. Then he'll kill you. If you want this to happen rather than lose that toe, why I may as well go back to your mother and sister. It is useless for me to stay here. There is no knowing when that trapper may come and he may have a terrible gun with him. A good hard pull with all your might will set you free. I'm going now. Come on!"

The young Otter shook his head. His eyes were filled with tears. He couldn't bear the thought of being left alone, yet he couldn't make up his mind to lose that toe. That toe was numb now. That trap didn't hurt so very much. But he was sure that if he should try to pull himself free, it would hurt dreadfully. It was because of this that he couldn't make up his mind to try.

"Good-by," said Little Joe Otter, and began to swim away swiftly. He didn't even look back. At first the young Otter couldn't believe that he was really being left alone. But his father kept straight on. Every second he was getting farther and farther away. At last the young Otter realized that his father had meant just what he said.

The young Otter stood it just as long as he could. Then the thought of being left alone in that cruel trap became more than he could bear. He plunged after his father. The trap brought him up short. But with all his might he struggled. He did n't even notice the pain. The thought of being left alone there was worse than any pain.

Suddenly that trap let go. At least he thought it had let go. He was free! I wish you could have seen him shoot through the water. How he did swim! Little Joe Otter heard him coming and waited for him. "So you decided that freedom is worth the price of a toe," said he.

Such a funny look as the face of that young Otter wore. It was not until then that he realized that he had left his toe behind.

CHAPTER XXX

THE OTTERS MOVE ON

Who doth the law of safety heed
Will not be influenced by greed.

Little Joe Otter.

THE young Otter, who had left a toe behind in a trap, was so happy to be free again that he hardly gave the loss of that toe a thought. The cold water was good for the sore foot, and as the young Otter was healthy, his foot healed rapidly. In fact, in two or three days his foot was practically well. But the young Otter did n't forget his dreadful experience.

He never would forget it. He had learned a lesson that he would remember as long as he lived. All his life he would be suspicious of traps and on the watch for them. Never again would that young Otter be caught in a trap.

Of course, the trapper found that toe in his trap. Such a disappointed trapper as he was! "There won't be a chance of catching that Otter again," said he. "I must have been careless in setting that trap. It should have caught him by the whole foot and not just by a toe. Probably those other Otters know all about it now."

When he discovered the new slippery slide he knew that his

traps at the old slippery slide had been found. He set another trap at the foot of the new slide, but he didn't have much hope of catching any one in it. He understood perfectly that Little Joe Otter and Mrs. Joe were wise in the ways of trappers. "I guess," muttered the trapper, "that my best chance of getting one of those Otters will be to hide for a chance to shoot one of them. To-morrow I'll spend the day over here with my gun."

So he spent all the next day hidden near the slippery slide, watching with his terrible gun. But he didn't have a chance to use it. He didn't get so much as a glimpse of a sleek, brown head.

And the reason was that Little Joe Otter and his family were far away down the brook. They had started early the night before. They were on their way down to the Big River.

Little Joe and Mrs. Joe had talked the matter all over. "It is n't safe to stay here any longer," declared Little Joe. "I don't like to leave the good fishing, for we may not find another place where it is so easy to get plenty of fish. But that terrible two-legged creature will give us no peace. There is a trap now at the foot of our new slippery slide."

"You are quite right, my dear," replied Mrs. Otter. "I am worried to death for fear, in spite of all their watchfulness, one of the children will get caught in a terrible trap and be killed. I think the sooner we move along the better. Safety is the most important thing."

So once more Little Joe and his family went traveling. There was a crust on the snow now, and they had a lot of fun sliding. Moreover, they didn't leave a trail as when they had left the Laughing Brook in the soft snow. They followed the big brook on its way towards the Big River. Now and then they came to open places where the water was swift and hadn't frozen. There they stopped to fish. Sometimes they swam for quite a distance under the ice.

CHAPTER XXXI

A FISH DISAPPEARS

*Before you boast be sure you know
That you have got the fish to show.*

Little Joe Otter.

AT the place where the big
brook, down which Little Joe
Otter and his family had traveled,
enters the Big River, the latter
never freezes over. Little Joe
Otter knew this. You see, he
had been there before more than
once. He knew that there was
good fishing in the Big River,
and that if no trapper discovered
them they would not be disturbed.
No men lived near that part of

the Big River. There was green forest on both banks. There were snug, dry, hiding-places, and Little Joe knew them all. They would stay until spring and then work down the Big River and so return to the Laughing Brook from which they had started.

The young Otters liked this place. They soon had a fine slippery slide on which to play when they were not sleeping or fishing. It was fun to explore under the ice along the banks of the Big River. It was fun to catch a fish and climb out on the ice to eat it. There was nothing to worry about. There were no enemies to fear. By day as well as by night they felt perfectly safe.

One day the young Otter who had lost his toe caught an extra big fish. It was the biggest fish he ever had caught. He was very proud of it as he climbed out on the ice. Now he had caught that fish more for the fun of catching it than because he was hungry. The fact is, he wasn't hungry. Fish were plentiful, and he had already eaten about all he could. So he merely took a couple of bites from what he considered the best part — just back of the head. Then he saw his sister over on the slippery slide and went over to join her, leaving the big fish on the ice. He wanted to tell her about that big fish. He wanted to boast a little.

He was sure that it was a bigger fish than she ever had caught. So when he got over to the slippery slide he at once began to boast. His sister stood it as long as she could. Then she declared that she did n't believe he had such a wonderful fish.

"Come on over and I'll show it to you," said the young Otter. "It's twice as big as any fish you've ever caught."

"I don't believe it," declared his sister. "I'll have to see it before I'll believe it."

"All right, come on!" cried her brother, and down the slippery slide he glided into the water. Flat on her stomach behind him went his sister. Together they

climbed out on the ice where the
big fish had been left.

"Here it — " began the young
Otter, and stopped abruptly.

"Well, where is it?" demanded
his sister.

Her brother simply stared all
about him with a foolish look on
his face. There was no fish there!
What could have become of it?
He knew that he had killed it
and so it could n't possibly have
flopped back into the water. He
ran all around with his nose to
the ice, but there was no scent
of Reddy Fox or of any one else.

"I don't believe you caught a
big fish," declared his sister.
"You must have dreamed it. If
you caught it, where is it?"

CHAPTER XXXII

THE LIVING HEAP OF SNOW

Don't think, but make quite sure you *know*
A thing is thus or mayhap so.

Little Joe Otter.

OF all the puzzled people in all
the Great World none was more
puzzled than was the young Otter
whose big fish had disappeared.
He had certainly killed that fish.
He had even taken two big bites
out of the choicest part of it. So
he knew that the fish could n't
have flopped off the ice into the
water while he was away. He
had been gone only a few minutes,

just long enough to get his sister
and bring her over to see that big
fish. He had boasted that it was
bigger than any fish she ever had
caught. Now there was n't a trace
of it anywhere.

His sister tossed her head. "I
don't believe you caught a big fish
at all," said she.

"But I tell you I did," protested
her brother. "I caught him and
I left it right here."

"Then where is it?" demanded
his sister.

But this the young Otter
could n't say. He wished he could.
He had a queer and most uncom-
fortable feeling. It made him
uneasy. Actually it made him
afraid. He did n't know what he

"WELL, SON," SAID HE, "WHAT DID YOU SEE?"
Page 196.

was afraid of, but he was afraid.
So when his sister disgustedly
plunged into the water and swam
back to the slippery slide on the
bank, he followed her.

But somehow he could n't enjoy
that slippery slide. He kept
thinking about that lost fish. To
make matters worse, his sister kept
teasing him about it. She called
him a boaster. It was clear that
she didn't believe he had caught
that big fish he had boasted about.
So after going down the slippery
slide a few times, he swam back to
the place where he had left the big
fish. He climbed out on the ice
and once more looked around
everywhere for signs of some one
who might have stolen that big

fish. But not a sign could he find.

A little way off on the ice was a little heap of snow. At least the young Otter thought it was a heap of snow. He looked at it carelessly two or three times. But he didn't go over to it. He wasn't interested in heaps of snow. The only thing of interest to him just then was what had become of that fish. It was very mysterious. He didn't like a mystery. His uneasiness increased, so after awhile he once more swam away. He wanted to ask his father or his mother what could have become of that fish, but he didn't. He was afraid he would be laughed at. He was afraid that they would n't believe he had caught it any more than his sister believed it.

Now hardly had that young Otter disappeared when what he had taken for a little heap of snow disappeared too. It disappeared without a sound. You see, it was alive. It really was n't a heap of snow at all. If the young Otter had seen it go, he might possibly have guessed what had become of his big fish. But he did n't see it go, and the next time he visited that place he did n't even notice that that little white heap was no longer there.

CHAPTER XXXIII

ANOTHER FISH DISAPPEARS

In things at once not understood
Some people will admit no good.

Little Joe Otter.

So many things happen every day to the little people of the Green Forest and the Green Meadows that they do not think of any one thing very long. Two days after the mysterious disappearance of his big fish the young Otter had stopped thinking about it. He had made up his mind that he never would know what became of that fish and that the matter was no longer worth puz-

zling over. There were too many
other things to think about and
do.

On the third day he caught
another fine fish and climbed out
on the ice with it near the place
where he had left the other. This
fish wasn't so big as the one
that had disappeared, but it was
a fine fish for all that. The young
Otter was hungry and he intended
to eat that fish right there. But
he had taken only a bite or two
when his sharp eyes saw another
fish in the water. Two fish would
be better than one. He dropped
on the ice the fish he was eating,
plunged into the water and like a
brown streak shot after the other
fish.

Swift as a fish is in water, there is n't much chance for it when once an Otter gets after it. The young Otter had quite a chase, but in the end he caught the fish. Then with it in his mouth he swam back and climbed out on the ice at the place where he had left the first fish. He was feeling very well satisfied. With two fish he would have all he could possibly eat, and more too.

"First I 'll eat the one that I caught first," said the young Otter, as he dropped on the ice the one he had just caught. Then he received a shock. That other fish was n't there! There was only one fish and that was the one he had just caught. He could n't believe it. No, Sir, he could n't believe it. He actually rubbed his eyes two or three times, to make sure that nothing was the matter with them. But nothing was the matter; that other fish wasn't there.

The young Otter hastily looked in every direction. No one was in sight. At least he didn't see any one. All he saw was what he took to be a little heap of snow a short distance away. He looked in the water. He thought he might have knocked that fish into the water when he dived after the other one. But he looked in vain.

Of course, right away he remembered the disappearance of the big fish a few days before. Now another had disappeared just as mysteriously. It was unbelievable, but it was true. The young Otter became frightened.

"This is no place for me," said he. "No, Sir, this is no place for me. The first thing I know, this fish will disappear right out of my mouth. I wouldn't mind losing the fish so much if I could only know what becomes of them."

He looked hastily down to see if the fish he had just caught was still at his feet. It was, and with a little sigh of relief he picked it up and with it in his mouth plunged into the water and swam hurriedly over to the bank. There he gulped that fish down as fast as ever he could. He did it as if he feared that it might disappear before he could get it eaten.

CHAPTER XXXIV

THE YOUNG OTTER LEARNS WHERE HIS FISH WENT

Each bit of knowledge you attain
Will prove an aid to future gain.
Little Joe Otter.

THE young Otter had told his father, Little Joe Otter, the story of how his fish had mysteriously disappeared. You should have seen the twinkle in Little Joe's eyes as he listened.

"Would you really like to know what became of your fish?" Little Joe asked.

"Of course I would," replied the

young Otter. "But I don't believe anybody will ever find out."

"Don't you think I could find
out if I went over there?" asked
Little Joe.

The young Otter shook his head
very decidedly. "No, I don't,"
said he very honestly.

"All right, son, let's go fishing,"
replied Little Joe Otter, his eyes
twinkling more than ever.

So together they went fishing,
and presently each caught a fish.
"You take yours over to the bank,
but don't stop to eat it. Keep
your eyes on this fish of mine,"
said Little Joe.

The young Otter obediently took
his fish over to the bank and then
sat down to watch. Little Joe

Otter climbed out on the ice at the place where the young Otter had twice lost his fish. He laid the fish down on the ice, then plunged into the water and swam over to where the young Otter was. Before he got there, the young Otter saw a great, broad-winged, white bird appear as if from nowhere, without stopping in his flight, pick up that fish on the ice and fly away a short distance. Then this great bird alighted on the ice and suddenly did n't look like a bird at all. He looked like just a little heap of snow. He looked exactly like the heap of snow that the young Otter had seen over there several times before.

You should have seen the eyes

of that young Otter pop out of his head. He was so surprised that for a full minute he couldn't find his tongue.

Little Joe Otter's eyes twinkled more than ever. "Well, son," said he, "what did you see?"

"I saw your fish disappear," gasped the young Otter. "Now I know where my fish went to. Do you see that little white heap over there that looks like snow?"

Little Joe Otter laughed right out. "Certainly I see it," said he. "I saw it as soon as we came over here. I saw it and I knew what it was. That is Whitey the Snowy Owl, who has come down from the Far North. He is very fond of fish. I guessed right away who had stolen your fish. Now we'll go over and see what he has to say about it."

So together they swam over and climbed out on the ice. Then they made right straight for Whitey. He turned his head, and the young Otter saw as fierce a pair of eyes as he had ever looked into. They were round and yellow. Whitey snapped and hissed. Then he turned so as to face them. He still clutched the fish in his claws. Little Joe Otter snarled and bounded towards him. Whitey hesitated only a second, then spread his broad wings and silently flew away, taking the fish with him. Little Joe was too big for him to fight with.

So it was the Young Otter made the acquaintance of Whitey the Snowy Owl, and learned that there is always an explanation for a mystery.

Enough is enough and I am sure you have heard enough of Little Joe Otter and his family. I could tell you much more, but it wouldn't be fair to some other little people in the Smiling Pool. And so the next book in the Smiling Pool series is to be about one whom you all know and, if you are like me, are fond of. It will be called Jerry Muskrat at Home.